Disney
Bambi

This edition published by Parragon Books Ltd in 2016

Parragon Books Ltd
Chartist House
15–17 Trim Street
Bath BA1 1HA, UK
www.parragon.com

ISBN 978-1-4723-7232-1

Printed in China

Disney
Bambi

Bath · New York · Cologne · Melbourne · Delhi
Hong Kong · Shenzhen · Singapore

One spring morning, there was
great excitement in the forest.
A new prince had been born.
His name was Bambi. He was
the son of a noble stag, the Great
Prince of the Forest.

When he woke, the little spotted
fawn saw happy smiling faces all
around him.

"My name's Thumper," said
a friendly rabbit. Bambi smiled.

It wasn't long before Bambi
was ready to explore the forest.
He made lots of new friends.

The forest is a
wonderful place!
Bambi thought
to himself.

One day, Bambi and Thumper were playing. Birds fluttered above their heads. Thumper pointed to one and said, "That's a bird."

Bambi repeated the word, "Bird!"

Then a butterfly fluttered by. Bambi called out, "Bird!"

"No," giggled Thumper, "that's a butterfly."

Bambi turned to a pretty flower and shouted, "Butterfly!"

Thumper laughed. "No," he cried, "that's a flower!"

Suddenly, a small
black-and-white
head appeared.
"Flower!" said Bambi.
"That's not a flower!"
Thumper laughed.
"He can call me Flower if he wants to," said the little
skunk. Bambi had made another new friend.

The days passed happily for Bambi. One morning his mother took him to a new place – the meadow.

The meadow was wide and open. Bambi's mother warned him that they had to be very careful. "There are no trees here to hide us," she said.

Bambi ran off to play. Soon, he found a pond. He leaned over and looked into the water at his own reflection.

Suddenly, another reflection appeared. It belonged to a female fawn about the same age as Bambi. She wanted to play.

Bambi felt very shy. He ran back to his mother and tried to hide.

"It's all right," Bambi's mother said. "That's Faline. She just wants to be your friend. Go and say hello."

Bambi went back to Faline. Soon, the two fawns were playing hide-and-seek in the tall grass.

Just then, a group of stags charged across the meadow, led by the Great Prince. He had come to warn the deer that there was danger nearby. All of the deer dashed towards the trees.

Later that day, Bambi asked his mother what the danger had been.

"Man was in the forest," she told him.

Summer and autumn passed and the weather grew
colder. One morning, Bambi awoke to find the world
had turned white.

"That's snow," his mother said. "Winter has come."

Bambi heard Thumper calling him. He found his
friend sliding across an icy pond.

"Come on, you can slide too!" called Thumper.

Bambi rushed over to join him. But he fell on his tummy with a loud **THUD!**

Thumper showed Bambi how to balance on the ice. Soon, Bambi was gliding across the pond too!

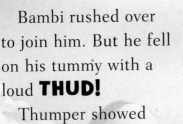

Winter was fun at first, but as time passed there was
less and less food. Eventually, there was nothing for Bambi
and his mother to eat except the bark on the trees.

One day, when it felt a little warmer, Bambi and his
mother went to the meadow to search for food. There they
found a small patch of green grass peeping out of the snow!
Bambi and his mother ate the grass hungrily.

Suddenly, Bambi's mother looked up and sniffed the air.
She sensed danger.

"Go back to the forest!" she told Bambi. "Quickly! Run!"

Bambi raced across the meadow with his mother behind
him. There was a loud – **BANG!**

"Faster, Bambi, and don't look back!" his mother shouted.

Bambi ran into the forest where it was safe.

Home at last, Bambi turned to look for his mother.
But she was not there. Bambi's heart thumped with
panic as he called for his mother again and again.
   The little fawn began to cry.

Just then, his father appeared by his side.

"Your mother cannot be with you any longer," he told Bambi gently. The Great Prince would now protect his son until he could look after himself.

As the months passed, Bambi and his friends grew up. One day, Flower met a female skunk and fell in love.

"Oh, no!" said Thumper. "Flower's twitterpated! Owl says it happens to everyone in the springtime!"

"It won't happen to me," Bambi said.

"Me neither," Thumper agreed.

Minutes later, Thumper met a female rabbit and he too was twitterpated!

Bambi wandered off
for a drink.

"Hello," said a soft
voice. It was Faline,
his childhood friend.

Faline licked Bambi's
face. He liked it. He'd
become twitterpated too!

But another young stag called Ronno also liked Faline. He challenged Bambi to a fight. Although Ronno was stronger, Bambi won! Bambi and Faline were free to begin their life together.

One autumn morning, Bambi was woken by a strange smell. He left Faline sleeping and went to investigate.

He climbed a cliff and saw smoke in the distance. Just then, his father came up beside him.

"Man has returned," he said. "We must go deep into the forest – quickly!"

Bambi rushed to warn Faline.

When Bambi arrived, he saw that a pack of angry dogs had trapped Faline on a cliff! Bambi rushed at the dogs and Faline escaped. Bambi fought them off and turned to follow Faline.
But suddenly, he heard a loud **BANG!**

Bambi felt a terrible pain and fell to the ground. He had been shot! Flames from man's campfire started to sweep towards him, but he couldn't move!

"Get up, Bambi," a voice said. It was Bambi's father.

The young Prince got to his feet and followed his father through the burning forest. They came to a waterfall and jumped. They crashed into the water far below and waded through the water towards an island.

Many other birds and animals had already found shelter on the island.

Faline was there too. She was overjoyed to see
Bambi again and gently licked his wounded shoulder.

Safe on the island, the forest creatures watched
helplessly as the fire destroyed their homes.

Only when the fire had finally burned out were
they able to return to the forest.

After a long winter, spring arrived.
The forest was beautiful once more.

One warm morning, all the animals and birds came to see
Faline and her two new fawns. Standing nearby was their
proud father, Bambi, the new Great Prince of the Forest.